Seymour Simon

PLANETS AROUND THE SUN

SeaStar Books · NEW YORK

This book is dedicated to my grandson Joel.

Special thanks to reading consultant Dr. Linda B. Gambrell, Director of the School of Education at Clemson University, past president of the National Reading Conference, and past board member of the International Reading Association.

Permission to use the following photographs is gratefully acknowledged:
Front cover, title page: Science Photo Library, Photo Researchers, Inc.; pages 2–3, 6–7, 14–17, 26–31: National Space Science Data Center; pages 8–9: The Team Leader, Prof. Bruce C. Murray and National Space Science Data Center; pages 10–11: Dr. Robert W. Carslon, The Galileo Project and National Space Science Data Center; pages 12–13: The Principal Investigator, Dr. Frederick J. Doyle and National Space Science Data Center; pages 18–25: The Team Leader, Dr. Bradford A. Smith and National Space Science Data Center.

First published in the United States by SEASTAR BOOKS, a division of NORTH-SOUTH BOOKS INC., New York. Published simultaneously in Canada, Australia, and New Zealand by North-South Books, an imprint of Nord-Süd Verlag AG, Gossau Zürich, Switzerland.

Library of Congress Cataloging-in-Publication Data is available.
ISBN 1-58717-145-7 (reinforced trade edition)
1 3 5 7 9 RTE 10 8 6 4 2
ISBN 1-58717-146-5 (paperback edition)
1 3 5 7 9 PB 10 8 6 4 2
PRINTED IN SINGAPORE BY TIEN WAH PRESS
For more information about our books, and the authors and artists who create them,
visit our web site: www.northsouth.com

we live on a planet called Earth.

Earth is one of nine planets
that travel around the sun.
The sun and everything
that travels around it
are called the solar system.

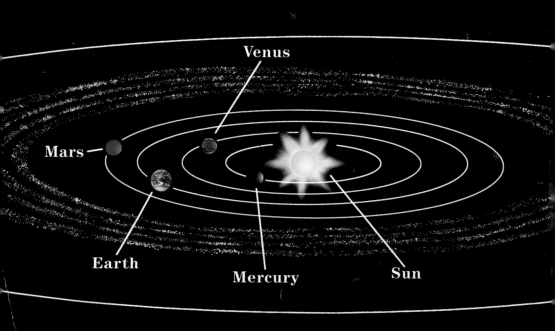

Venus

Mars

Earth

Mercury

Sun

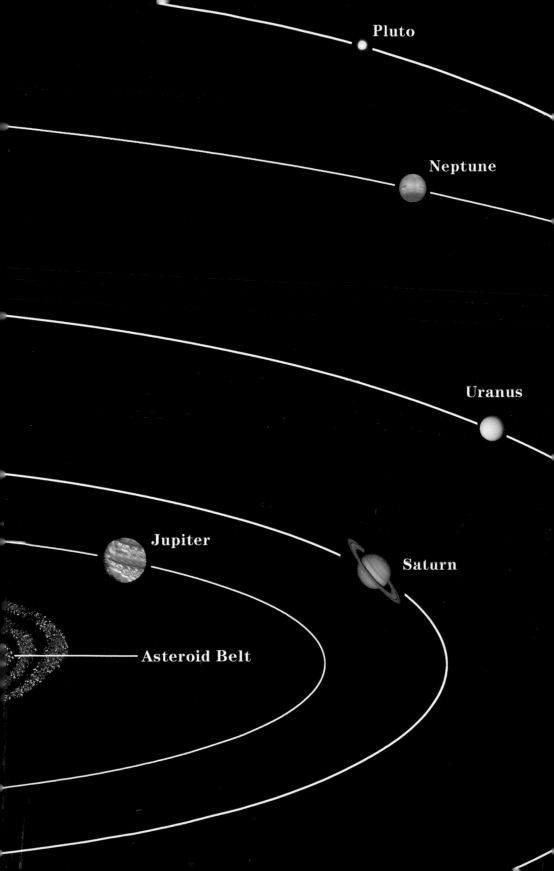

Pluto

Neptune

Uranus

Jupiter

Saturn

Asteroid Belt

The sun is a giant ball

of fiery hot gases.

If Earth were the size

of a basketball,

the sun would be as big

as a basketball court.

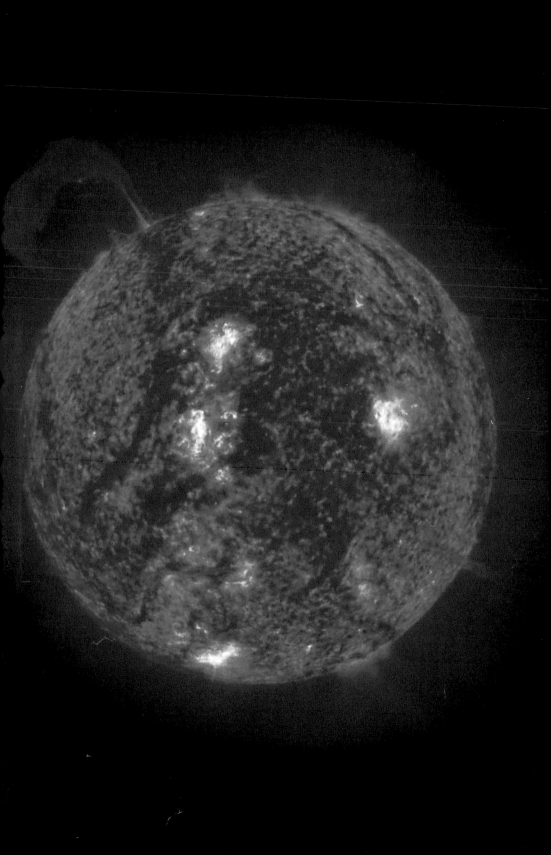

Mercury is closest to the sun.

During the day, its temperature

is almost 800 degrees.

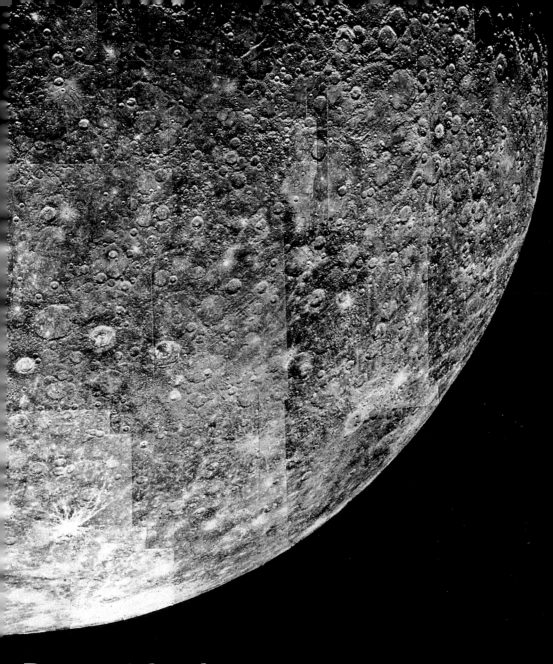

But at night, the temperature

drops to nearly 300 degrees

below zero.

Venus is about the same size
as Earth, but it is very different.

Thick clouds cover the planet
but it has no water.

Venus is the hottest planet
in our solar system.

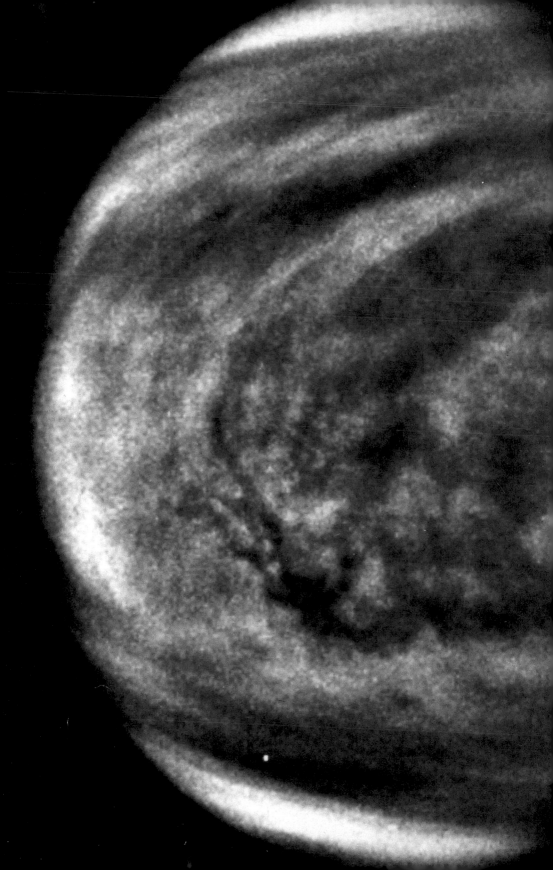

Earth is the only planet
that has water on its surface.

If Earth were closer to the sun,

the oceans would boil away.

If it were farther away,

the oceans would freeze.

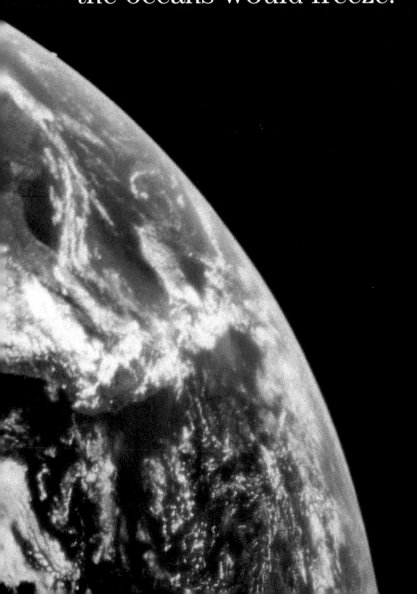

Earth's moon is not a planet.

Planets travel around the sun.

Moons travel around planets.

Even though Earth's moon

is 250,000 miles away,

it is our closest neighbor.

**Phases
of the
Moon**

new moon

crescent moon

quarter moon

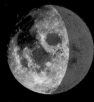

gibbous moon

full moon

The surface of Mars is
a red, dusty soil.
Spacecraft from Earth
have landed on Mars.

People are interested in
looking for signs of life there.
But so far they have found
no signs of life.

Jupiter is much larger than all of the other planets combined.

The surface of Jupiter is an ocean of liquid hydrogen 10,000 miles deep.

The Great Red Spot is a giant storm on Jupiter.

This storm is bigger than Earth.

Saturn is the second largest planet.

Saturn has rings made

of pieces of ice, rock, and dust.

Some pieces are smaller
than a dime.
Others are as big as a house.

Uranus is a green planet.

Its very thin rings are made

of an unknown black material.

Uranus has 5 large moons

and at least 16 smaller ones.

Neptune is a blue-green planet with giant storms on its surface. Freezing winds blow across Neptune at speeds of up to 700 miles per hour.

Pluto is the coldest planet.

It is a distant ball

of frozen gases and rock.

Some scientists think it is

too small to be called a planet.

But most people still call

Pluto the ninth planet

of our solar system.

Asteroids are
chunks of rock.
They are much
smaller than planets.
About 4,000 asteroids
circle the sun between
Mars and Jupiter.
This area is called
the asteroid belt.

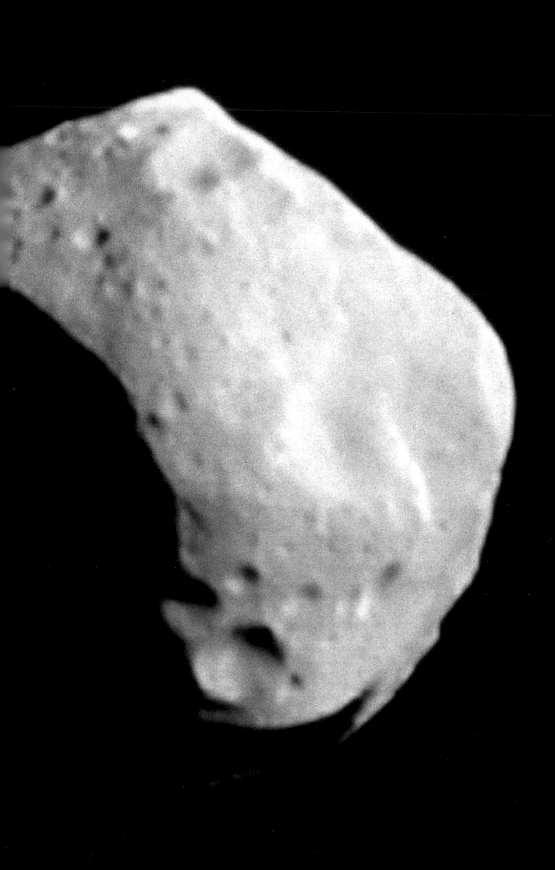

Far out in space, other planets circle other stars.

But no one knows if any distant planets are like Earth. We still have much to learn about planets and stars.

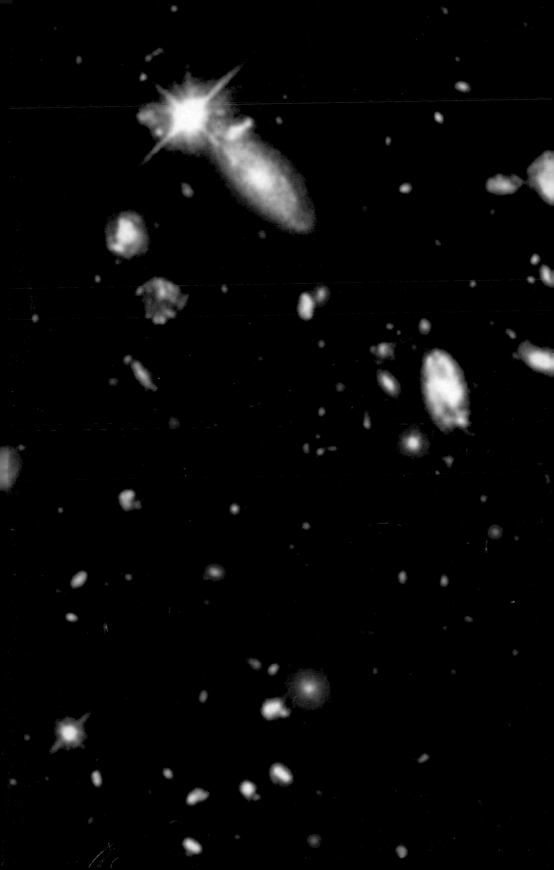

	Mercury	Venus	Earth	Mars	Jupiter	Saturn	Uranus	Neptune	Pluto
Distance from Sun (millions of miles)	36	67	93	142	484	891	1785	2793	3647
Orbital Period (days)	88	225	365	687	4331	10,747	30,589	59,800	90,588
Diameter (miles)	3032	7521	7926	4222	88,846	74,897	31,763	30,775	1485
Length of Day (hours)	4223	2802	24	25	10	11	17	16	153
Average Temperature (F)	333	867	59	-85	-166	-220	-320	-330	-375
Moons	0	0	1	2	28	30	21	8	1
Rings	No	No	No	No	Yes	Yes	Yes	Yes	No